SKOKIE PUBLIC LIBRARY
3 1232 00965 0161

D1171331

MARYA KHAN
AND THE
SPECTACULAR FALL FESTIVAL
TICKET
TICKET

THE MARYA KHAN SERIES

Book 1: Marya Khan and the Incredible Henna Party

Book 2: Marya Khan and the Fabulous Jasmine Garden

Book 3: Marya Khan and the Spectacular Fall Festival

AMULET BOOKS • NEW YORK

MARYA KHAN AND THE SPECTACULAR FALL FESTIVAL

written by
SAADIA FARUQI

illustrated by
ANI BUSHRY

PUBLISHER'S NOTE: This is a work of fiction. Names, characters, places, and incidents are either the product of the author's imagination or used fictitiously, and any resemblance to actual persons, living or dead, business establishments, events, or locales is entirely coincidental.

Cataloging-in-Publication Data has been applied for and may be obtained from the Library of Congress.

ISBN 978-1-4197-6120-1

Book design by Deena Micah Fleming

Printed and bound in U.S.A.
10 9 8 7 6 5 4 3 2 1

ABRAMS The Art of Books
195 Broadway, New York, NY 10007
abramsbooks.com

FOR
MUBASHIR
AND
MARIAM

1

EXPERTISE

Special knowledge or skill

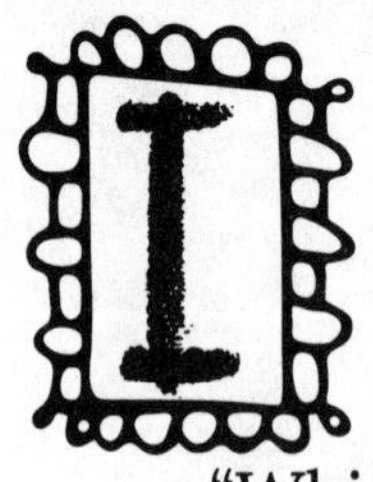

loved pumpkins. Big round ones. Little cutie-pie ones. Pumpkins were the best veggie on planet Earth.

"Which one should we get, Marya?" Baba asked me.

I squinted, because it made me look like a pumpkin expert. Also, because the sun was in my eyes. "That one!" I pointed to a big orange ball in the middle of the pumpkin patch.

"That's old," Sal said. "See, the skin is wrinkled."

Wait, did my brother think he was an expert too?

Nope. No way. Being in fifth grade didn't make you all-knowing. "That's how all the pumpkins are," I told him. "Right, Baba?"

Baba looked around like he was trying to run away from us. Or maybe he was just admiring our town's pumpkin patch. It was gigantic!

"Baba?"

Baba coughed. "Ahem, I think . . ."

Just then, I spied an even bigger and better pumpkin. "Wow, that one!" I yelled. I ran and put my arms around it so nobody else would buy it. "Please, Baba! This one!"

Sal ran up and patted it. "This is perfect!" he said.

I rolled my eyes. I knew what he was doing. Showing off his expertise. That was a word from my Word of the Day diary, and it didn't fit my brother, like, at all. In fact, he had the complete opposite of expertise. He had no-knowledge-ise.

Only that's not a real word, sadly.

"Are you sure, Marya?" Baba asked, frowning. "It may be too big for our car."

I nodded very fast. "Yup, this is the one. We can always put it in Mama's van."

Mama owned a flower shop, and she used a dusty old van to cart her plants and fertilizer around town. Fertilizer was made of poop, in case you didn't know. I knew, because when it accidentally spilled on me one time, I smelled like poop for the whole day. My enemy/neighbor Alexa R. made fun of me in school and told everyone about it.

I didn't like Alexa R., basically. She was annoying and rich and always trying to be my friend.

"Marya Khan, is that you?" came an annoying voice from behind me.

Please don't be Alexa. Please don't be Alexa, I prayed very hard before turning around.

Only it didn't work, because the person standing behind me was definitely Alexa R. She was wearing a long pink party dress with glittering sequins. Plus, fancy pink shoes and a pink ribbon in her long blond hair. She looked perfect.

And very annoying.

Also, the pink hurt my eyes, so I glared at her.

"Why are you dressed like that? This is a pumpkin patch, not a party."

She swished her hair. "My mom says one must always look one's best."

"One's best what?"

Alexa frowned. "I'm not sure. I think it means always dress in your best clothes."

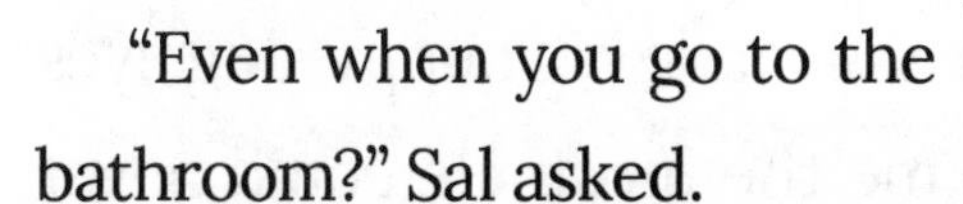

"Even when you go to the bathroom?" Sal asked.

"Ew, gross!" Alexa and I said together.

"What? You said *always* dress in your best clothes. That includes the bathroom, right?" Sal grinned. "And when you go to sleep? And when—"

Baba held up a hand. "Okay, that's enough, Sal." He looked at Alexa. "Hello, dear. Is your dad with you? I should go say hi."

Alexa looked at her shoes like they were the most interesting thing. "Um, no. He's on a business trip."

Again? It seemed like Alexa's dad was always taking trips.

"Never mind," Baba said, smiling kindly. "Maybe next time."

Alexa looked up and saw my pumpkin. The huge, shiny, amazing one. "Wow," she breathed. "Are you getting that one, Marya?"

I nodded proudly. "Yup."

"I don't think we need such a big one," Baba protested.

I caught his arm and made big puppy-dog eyes at him. Baba loved me the most. He could never resist my puppy-dog eyes. "Baba, please? Imagine

how much pumpkin bread we could make with this."

By "we" I meant "Mama." She was an expert at cooking yummy things. Every year, after Baba, Sal, and I brought home the biggest pumpkin we could find, she scooped out the insides and made all sorts of delicious food. Pumpkin curry. Pumpkin cookies. Pumpkin bread. Pumpkin soup.

Okay, that last one was yucky, but everything else was really delicious. Especially the bread.

I guess Baba was also thinking about Mama's amazing cooking, because he sighed and said, "Okay, you win."

"Yay!" I cried. It was no surprise, though. I always won with Baba.

He left with Sal to talk to the pumpkin patch owner. I stood next to my pumpkin to guard it. A lady in a big hat walked over to check it out. "That one's mine!" I told her loudly.

She gave me a dirty look and went away.

"No need to be so rude, Marya," Alexa said. "My mom says you can catch more flies with honey than vinegar."

I wrinkled my nose. "What are you talking about? There aren't any flies here."

"It means you should be nice to people."

"Your mom has a lot of weird sayings," I grumbled. Alexa's mom was on the city council and always running around looking very important. Right now, she was standing near the fence, talking to someone.

"Yeah," Alexa replied. She looked down at her shoes again, like she was sad.

Ugh. Even though I technically didn't like her, I had to cheer her up. I didn't like sad people even more. "Don't you just love the fall?" I said brightly.

Alexa looked up and blinked. "Yes! I love trees with orange leaves!"

I was thinking more about pumpkin pie, but orange leaves were also cool. "Me too!" I agreed.

Just then, two things happened. First, there was a very loud announcement. "The party dress competition is about to begin. All contestants, please report to the front desk!"

Er, party dress competition?

Second, Alexa's mom turned to us and waved her arms. "Alexa!" she screeched. "Come on!"

Okay, I guess the all-pink outfit made more sense now. Alexa flipped her perfect blond hair. She didn't look sad anymore. She looked like she was the Queen of England and everyone was her servant. "Watch me win, Marya," she said, and walked away.

And guess what? She totally won the party dress competition.

I just stood there in my plain blue jeans and white T-shirt with my mouth wide open and watched her take the pumpkin-shaped trophy.

2

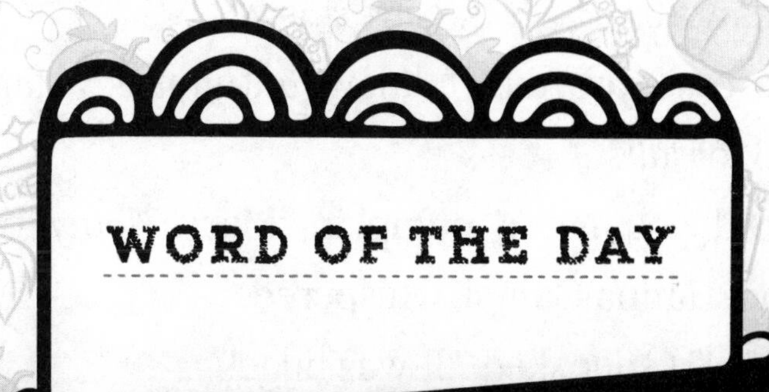

WORD OF THE DAY

FEROCIOUS

Very scary-looking

At school on Monday, everybody was in fall mode. Our teacher, Miss Piccolo, was wearing a brown sweater with the words AUTUMN IS MY FAVORITE SEASON.

In case you didn't know, *autumn* is a fancy word for *fall*.

"Did you get a pumpkin, Marya?" my best friend, Hanna Gamal, whispered.

"Yes!" I squeaked. "It was huge!"

Miss Piccolo frowned at me. "Marya, will you please stop talking? I'm trying to take attendance."

I slumped in my seat. "Sorry," I said.

Right in front of me, Alexa sat very straight. She was wearing another fancy dress, only this time it was brown with white polka dots. I tried not to think about her taking home the pumpkin trophy on Saturday.

I wanted to stomp my foot. Why didn't I ever get a trophy for anything? Okay, I didn't have fancy clothes, but surely there was something else I could win at?

Miss Piccolo droned on and on while she took attendance. I wasn't listening. Maybe Alexa could help me find something to win at. Which meant I had to be nice to her. "Look, Alexa." I nudged her with my foot. "The tree outside has orange leaves."

"I know!" Alexa whispered without looking up.

"Why are you talking about leaves?" Hanna asked, frowning.

Oops! I hadn't told Hanna that I'd met Alexa at the pumpkin patch. "I'll tell you later," I promised.

Miss Piccolo stood up and put her hands on

her hips. "Marya Khan! What did I tell you about talking?"

Double oops. I slumped even lower in my seat.

She walked right up to my desk. Actually, it was a square made up of four desks pushed together. Mine, Hanna's, and Alexa's. Plus, an empty desk that nobody sat at. "What were you talking about?" Miss Piccolo asked.

"Um, nothing," I said.

Okay, I basically lied. Only I prefer to call it

protecting myself from evil witches disguised as teachers.

"Really?" Miss Piccolo raised an eyebrow. It totally meant she didn't believe me. Drat.

"We were talking about fall, Miss Piccolo," Alexa answered. "I love pumpkins, don't you?"

I gave Alexa a ferocious glare. That meant a glare so big I probably looked like a lion or tiger or something. First of all, because she told on me. And second of all, because I'm the one who loves pumpkins the most. Not her.

Alexa was always stealing things from me. Not real things, but ideas. Like the time she wanted to be garden leader, just like me. And the time she got to the school library first and borrowed a book I really wanted to read. And the time—

"Fall, huh?" Miss Piccolo nodded. I waited for her to scold us. Instead, she smiled. "Perfect topic for today, girls."

Hanna and I exchanged looks. "What do you mean, Miss Piccolo?" I asked.

Miss Piccolo went back to her desk. "I have

some good news." She put her arms up over her head like the football guys do on TV when they score a touchdown. "It's fall! Yay!"

Hanna giggled.

Antonio copied Miss Piccolo, only his "yay!" was really a yell. He loved football. And baseball. Basically, any game that was played outside.

My mouth dropped open. Miss Piccolo looked happy, but also a little weird. I didn't know teachers did *yay!* touchdowns.

"Our school is planning a fall festival!" Miss

Piccolo continued. "There will be games and food, even a hayride!"

Okay, now the touchdown made sense. Everyone got excited. A few of the girls squealed. Omar whooped.

"That's amazing!" Antonio practically yelled.

Alexa turned to me. "See, Marya? Everybody loves fall," she said smugly.

I rolled my eyes. "They just want the food and games."

"Don't forget the hayride!" Hanna added.

I opened my eyes wide, because I'd never been on a hayride before. It was one of my big dreams in life.

"Oh, hayrides are awesome!" Alexa gushed, because of course she's been on so many. Probably hundreds. She was probably a hayride expert.

She'd probably gotten trophies for best hayride riding while wearing pretty dresses.

"Have you been on a hayride before?" Hanna asked Alexa.

Alexa nodded. "Oh yes. We go to my grandfather's farm every Thanksgiving. It's got horses and cows and tractors . . ."

I scowled and crossed my arms over my chest, because I didn't want to know about Alexa's grandparents' amazing farm.

I focused on Miss Piccolo. "Each class will get a

table at the festival," she said. "We have to decide on a fun activity for our table."

"Like what?" Antonio asked.

"Anything you like. A game. A food stall. The sky's the limit."

"What does that mean?" Omar asked.

Miss Piccolo looked surprised. "Oh, it means you can do anything as long as it's allowed. Anything fun."

"Like fart cushions?" Antonio said, laughing. Omar snorted loudly.

Miss Piccolo was not amused. "No."

Then she said something that made me sit up straight. "Each of you will be asked to sell tickets to the festival. All the money we raise will go to charity. The student who raises the most money will get a special prize from Principal Cleveland."

I froze. A special prize? Like a trophy?

This was the answer to all my prayers.

Of course, this had to be the job for me! I was *dying* to win something! It didn't even matter what I won, just that I did.

Everyone would think I was amazing. I'd finally be way better than Alexa, with her fancy clothes and sparkly backpack that her dad had gotten her from Paris. And especially her grandparents' farm that had hayrides.

I imagined Miss Piccolo giving me a certificate. Or maybe a medal. We'd have a special ceremony in the cafeteria. Even Principal Cleveland would be there. And of course, my whole family would come to watch me win. A band would play music, and confetti would shower over my head.

Miss Piccolo would cry happy tears because her favorite student had won the most for charity.

That would be me: Marya Khan.

I grinned and rubbed my hands together. It was time for me to be the winner.

It was time for Operation Sell Tickets.

3

WORD OF THE DAY

EXTRAORDINARY

Very unusual and remarkable

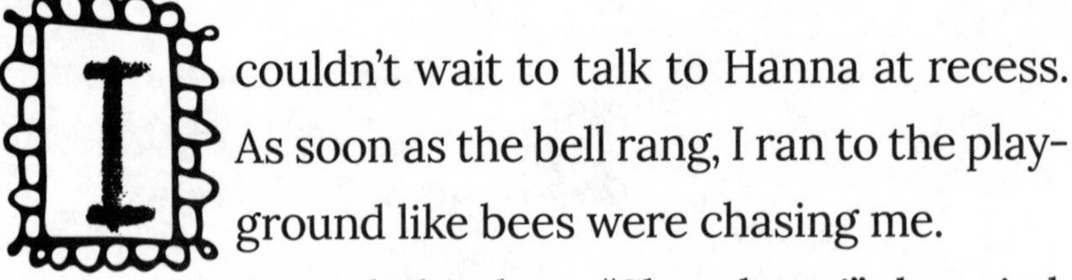

I couldn't wait to talk to Hanna at recess. As soon as the bell rang, I ran to the playground like bees were chasing me.

Hanna ran behind me. "Slow down!" she cried.

"No time!" I cried back, panting.

"For what?"

I didn't reply. I was running out of air. I reached the bench we usually sat on and practically collapsed onto it. "Phew!"

Hanna sat down next to me. "What's the hurry?" she asked.

"I want to win the ticket thing!" I told her. "I've decided."

"What ticket thing?"

I couldn't believe she'd already forgotten. Miss Piccolo had gone on and on about how important the tickets were. The more I sold, the bigger my prize would be. Or something.

I had to admit I wasn't really listening to everything our teacher was saying.

"The tickets for the fall festival," I reminded

Hanna. "I want to make sure I sell the most. So I can win the prize."

Hanna frowned. "I think you missed the point, Marya. The tickets are to raise money for charity. The more tickets we sell, the more money we can give to the charity."

Oh yes, the charity. Miss Piccolo had told us about it. "All proceeds from the festival will go to the animal shelter," she'd said in class.

Proceeds mean *money*, in case anyone was wondering. My third-grade class wasn't good at big words, so I'm sure everyone was wondering.

Not me. I'm an expert on big words.

Hanna was watching me carefully. "Right, Marya?" she asked. "The tickets are for charity."

I knew that. Sort of. "Er, yes," I said. "The more tickets I sell, the more I raise for the animals."

She patted me on the back like she was saying good job. "Yes!"

"And to win the prize," I added.

"Sure, whatever you say." Hanna turned her head and gazed longingly at the swings. They were blue, with long twisty chains made of shiny metal. "Can we go play now?"

"I don't have time to play, Hanna!" I whined. "I have to come up with a plan."

"A plan?"

I looked around to make sure nobody was listening. Then I leaned forward and whispered in her ear: "Operation Sell Tickets."

She let out a giggle. "Seriously?"

I glared at her. "Yes, seriously. What is this, comedy hour?"

Hanna giggled again. But she must have realized that I wasn't joking. She gave one last look at the swings, then sighed. "Okay. I'll help you."

I sat back, relieved. If Hanna helped me, I'd sell more tickets. I'd win for sure.

Then I thought of something bad. "Wait, if you help me, that means you can't win yourself."

Hanna rolled her eyes. "I don't care about winning. I just want to raise money for the animal shelter. I love animals."

This was true. Hanna's entire family were animal lovers. They had three birds, one rabbit, and a turtle. Still, she was wrong about one thing. "You don't care about winning?" I said loudly. "How are we best friends?"

Hanna shrugged. "We just are."

"But—"

"Besides," Hanna continued, "we don't even know what the prize is. It could be something boring, like a gift card to that burger place nobody likes."

I shook my head. Nope. The prize was going to be something amazing. I just knew it. "It doesn't matter," I told her. "I still want to win."

She shrugged. "Okay."

Then I thought of something else. "You can't tell anyone," I said. "It has to be a secret."

"Why?"

I threw up my hands. "Because I don't want someone else to get the same idea."

"What idea?" came a very annoying voice from behind me. It was Alexa, of course.

I jumped. "Why do you keep sneaking up on me?" I almost yelled.

"Tell me what you were talking about," Alexa demanded.

I crossed my arms and tapped my foot. Why should I tell her? She'd only steal my idea and win instead of me. She was always doing sneaky things like that. "Nothing," I muttered.

Hanna said quickly, "Marya wants to sell a whole lot of tickets for the fall festival so she can win the prize."

My eyes bugged out. "That was a secret, Hanna!" I yelled.

Hanna's shoulders slumped. "Oh, sorry. I forgot."

"I want to win too," said Alexa.

I stomped my foot very hard. "You—"

Hanna clapped. "May the best girl win," she said.

"That will be me!" I said. I pointed at my chest. "I'm the best girl."

Alexa smiled a beautiful smile. "Maybe we can both win, Marya," she said way too sweetly. "Like co-winners."

Ugh. Alexa and her stupid ideas. Without answering, I got up from the bench and stomped away.

When we got back to class, I raised my hand very high. "Miss Piccolo?"

Our teacher sighed. "Yes, Marya?"

I gulped, because this was a big deal. "Um, what's the prize for selling the most tickets?"

She looked down her nose at me. "Are you still thinking about the festival, Marya?" she asked. "Surely there are more important things to think about. Like homework. Or the social studies test coming up on Friday."

I stared at her. How could she say that? The fall festival was super important. It was when I'd show everyone what a big winner I was. Plus, there would be games and food, and hopefully lots and lots of pumpkins.

Alexa raised her hand. "The festival is important because it will help the animal shelter, Miss Piccolo."

Oh yeah, that too.

Miss Piccolo smiled. "You're right, Alexa!"

I sent Alexa one of my ferocious looks for interrupting. "So, the prize?" I asked Miss Piccolo. "What is the prize for selling the most tickets?"

She pursed her lips. "Hmm, I'm not sure. Principal Cleveland hasn't told us yet."

"I think it will be free ice cream for a year," Omar said, licking a pretend ice cream cone.

I shook my head, because nope. Ice cream was too ordinary. The prize was going to be extraordinary. I knew it.

"Season tickets to baseball games," Antonio said.

"Or a spa day," Alexa chimed in.

Antonio groaned. "Only if you're a girl."

"Boys can go to the spa too," Alexa replied with a scowl. "There's no rule against it."

I didn't want to go to a spa. It sounded way too boring to me. I also didn't like baseball. "I think it will be a beach vacation," I said dreamily. I could just imagine it: bright sunshine, blue waves, maybe a Jet Ski or something. Oh, and those little coconuts with straws in them. I always wanted to try one of those.

4

PISTACHIO

A small green nut

with a tan shell

After school, I rushed to Dadi's room. She was Baba's mom, and she lived with us. Her room was my favorite place in the house. It had the comfiest bed, and always smelled of Vicks.

Okay, most people think Vicks is gross, but not me. It reminds me of this one time in first grade when I was sick. I got to stay home for three days, snuggled in Dadi's bed watching Urdu dramas and doing zero chores.

Dadi had put Vicks on my chest every day, and told me it was a miracle cure.

I got three days off from school, so it was definitely a miracle!

"Salaam, Marya!" Dadi was sitting on her bed, eating a bowl of pistachios. She smiled when she saw me. "How was your day?"

I climbed onto the bed and picked up a pistachio. It still had the shell on, but that was okay. Pistachio shells were super easy to break open. "I got a hundred on my English assignment," I reported. “And math was boring, because I knew all the answers already.”

“You’re such a good student.” Dadi patted my head.

Normally, I hated people patting my head. It made me feel like a baby. But when Dadi did it, I felt good, like she was telling me she loved me. “I know,” I replied, grinning. “I’m the best student, even better than Alexa.”

“Really?” Dadi didn’t look too sure.

“Okay, fine!” I ate some more pistachios. “We’re both the best.”

This was sad, but true. Alexa got the same score as me in almost every subject. We were even the same at rocket math, my very favorite thing in school. That's why I really needed Operation Sell Tickets. I was going to show Alexa that I was better than she was at something.

"I know you're the best, because you're my granddaughter," Dadi said. "That makes you special."

I sighed and flopped back onto the pillows. Being special to Dadi was old news. She'd loved me since the day I was born, probably. "I want to be special in school too!" If I'd been standing up, I would have stomped my foot to show her how serious I was.

Dadi pulled me up by my arm and kissed my forehead. "I'm sure you are. Now go switch on the TV. I want to watch my Urdu drama."

I spent the afternoon in my room, dreaming about the fall festival. I thought about the pumpkins and the face painting. But mostly, I thought about what I'd get if I sold the most tickets. That beach vacation sounded like heaven.

In the evening, I went down to the kitchen. Mama was making roti for dinner.

I wrinkled my nose. "Is there any spaghetti?"

Spaghetti was my favorite. Roti was not.

Mama looked at me sternly. "You should eat whatever's on the table, Marya."

"Yeah," my big sister, Aliyah, scoffed. "Stop being a little princess."

I scowled at her. She was thirteen years old and thought she knew everything. "I'm not a princess," I told her slowly. "Your parents have to be a king and a queen to be a princess."

Aliyah scowled back. Then she hissed like a snake. It was her signature sound. "I know! I'm just making a joke."

She looked angry, and not at all like she was joking. I'm pretty sure she didn't know what a joke was. But I wasn't about to tell her. She'd bite my head off.

Sal was sitting at the table, doing his homework. "If Marya's a princess, then I'm Prince Charming," he said.

I rolled my eyes. "You wish!"

"Stop arguing, you two," Mama interrupted. "Marya, there's no spaghetti today. If you finish all your roti with the chicken curry, you can have pumpkin cake for dessert."

I did a little happy jump. "Pumpkin cake! Hooray!"

Aliyah shook her head. "It's just cake, Marya. You don't have to freak out."

"It's not just cake," I insisted. "It's made of pumpkins, which are delicious!"

Dadi shuffled into the room. "What about pistachio cake?" she asked. "That would be delicious too."

Wow. I didn't know you could put pistachios in a cake. I licked my lips, imagining what it would taste like. Would it be green? Would the flavor be sweet or nutty? "Can you make pistachio cake tomorrow?" I asked Mama. "Pretty please?"

Mama shook her head. "I still have that huge pumpkin you brought home the other day."

When we started eating dinner, Baba said, "I got an email from your school today, Marya and Sal."

I quickly swallowed a piece of roti. "What about?" I asked nervously.

"About a fall festival," he replied. "Sounds like fun!"

I heaved a big sigh of relief. "Yes! It's at the end of the month. Only we have to sell tickets before then. To raise money for charity."

"Sounds like a scam," Aliyah said.

I gave her my most ferocious lion-glare. "It's charity! Only a witch would say charity is a scam!"

"Mama!" Aliyah wailed. "Marya's calling me names."

Everyone turned to stare at me.

“Marya!” Mama scolded me. “Don’t call your sister a witch!”

“Sorry,” I said, only I didn’t sound sorry at all. What sort of person makes fun of raising money for charity? A witch, that’s who.

I decided to change the subject. “Also, guess what?” I said brightly. “Whoever sells the most tickets wins a prize!”

“You think you’ll win?” Sal howled with laughter. “Not in a million years!”

I kicked him under the table. “I will too!”

“Ow,” he said loudly. “Mama, Marya kicked me.”

I opened my mouth to say something, but Mama gave me a ferocious look of her own. “Marya, if you don’t behave, you won’t get any cake today. Not even a crumb.”

Yikes! She was being serious. I quickly went back to my chicken curry. “Sorry,” I whispered. I knew I was acting bad. I think the stress of Operation Sell Tickets was getting to me.

5

WORD OF THE DAY

PREPARATION

The act of getting ready

The next morning, Miss Piccolo asked us for ideas for our festival table. Everyone raised their hands faster than speeding bullets. Alexa held up a notebook with a long list written in purple pen. "I'm ready, Miss Piccolo," she sang.

Miss Piccolo fiddled with something on her computer. "Give me a minute, class."

I looked at Alexa's pretty cursive handwriting. "What's that?" I whispered.

"I like to be prepared, Marya Khan," Alexa whispered back. "Preparation is the key to success."

I sat up straight. Did Alexa have a Word of

the Day diary too? “How’d you know those big words?” I asked suspiciously.

Alexa shrugged. “My mom says it all the time on the phone.”

I stared at her. “What does your mom do exactly?”

Alexa giggled. “I’m not sure. She works on the city council, but what she does there is a big mystery to me.”

“You never asked her?” This was unbelievable. I knew everything about Mama’s flower business, thanks to the smelly van I sat in every day. I knew less about Baba’s job, but at least I knew he was a manager in an office full of computers.

Alexa sighed and looked down at her notebook. “Not really,” she replied sadly. “Mom doesn’t have much time to talk. She’s always working.”

“She was at the pumpkin patch on Saturday,” I pointed out.

“Only because she’d entered me in that party dress competition.” Alexa looked out the window like she was remembering something. “She bought that dress from London, you know. Overnight delivery and everything."

"It looked nice," I said awkwardly.

Alexa looked at me and rolled her eyes. "Yeah, right."

I frowned. "I'm telling the truth," I insisted. "I'm not a liar."

Well, I mostly wasn't. Sometimes I had no other choice, like the time I broke the big china vase in our living room and told Mama a cat had gotten inside the house. Mama loved cats, so she didn't get mad.

Only now she left a plate of milk on the porch every night for a cat that didn't exist.

"Thanks," Alexa whispered. "That means a lot, Marya."

"Okay, class, let's get started." Miss Piccolo wrote *Fall Festival Ideas* on the whiteboard.

"We could have a bake sale," Hanna suggested.

"Boring!" Antonio called out from the back of the class.

I secretly agreed with him, but I kept my

mouth shut because Hanna was my best friend. Miss Piccolo wrote *Bake Sale* on the board.

"We need something amazing," Alexa said. "Something unique."

"How about mini golf?" Omar asked. "That's unique."

My mouth dropped open, because how would we set up a mini golf course at our school? "Get serious," I told Omar.

He just made a face at me. How rude.

"I know," Antonio shouted. "Ring toss!"

Miss Piccolo wrote that on the board too. She was smiling. I remembered how she did the *yay!* touchdown the day before. I guessed she was looking forward to the festival too.

"Ooh, a scavenger hunt," Alexa said, snapping her fingers.

I didn't want to tell her that sounded awesome, so I kept quiet. Again. Only I was getting tired of staying quiet, so I said, "How about face painting?"

"Oh, good idea, Marya!" Alexa said, clapping her hands.

"Who would be the painter?" Omar asked.

"Hanna," I replied quickly. "She's great at art."

Hanna blushed, but everyone started clapping because it was true. Hanna's art was amazing. She'd once painted a picture of George Washington that looked so real, Principal Cleveland put it on the school website.

"I think we have enough ideas," Miss Piccolo

said. She took a vote on the best idea. Turned out that face painting was everyone's favorite.

"Hooray!" I said.

Okay, maybe I yelled. It felt a little bit like winning, because my idea was chosen.

It wasn't a beach vacation or anything, but it still felt great.

Hanna got to be in charge of the stall, since it was art-related. "I'll ask my uncle to donate supplies from his art store," she said.

Miss Piccolo tapped the marker on the board. "Now that we've decided what our class is going to do," she said, "we need to talk about the most important part of the festival."

I sat up very straight. I knew exactly what was coming. "Tickets," I said.

Miss Piccolo nodded. "You don't need tickets to get into the festival, but you need them to buy things or play games," she explained.

Interesting. That meant each person would need a bunch of tickets if they wanted to have fun. "Perfect," I whispered.

Miss Piccolo handed me a plastic box. "Take a stack of tickets and pass the box to your neighbor, please."

I peered into the box. Stacks of pink tickets wrapped in plastic lay inside in neat rows. I took out one stack. "They look like movie stubs," I muttered.

Alexa took the box from me. “How many are in a stack, Miss Piccolo?” she asked.

“Good question, Alexa,” Miss Piccolo said.

Alexa beamed. “Thanks!”

“There are one hundred tickets in a stack,” Miss Piccolo continued. “Each ticket costs a dollar.”

The whole class said, “Ooh!” because let’s face it, that was *a lot* of tickets!

I clicked my fingers. “One dollar multiplied by a hundred,” I said loudly. “That means a hundred dollars if we sell the whole stack.”

This time, there was not a single *ooh*. In fact, everyone was super quiet. A hundred tickets was a lot for third graders.

I didn’t even know what a hundred dollars looked like.

“Just try your best,” Miss Piccolo said. “Nobody’s asking you to sell all hundred tickets. But if you do,” she added, “you can always come to me for more.”

I scoffed. “I can do it!”

Alexa crossed her arms over her chest. "Me too!" she said.

We eyed each other. There was no way I'd lose to Alexa again. She may have had the fanciest dresses, but selling tickets was a very different game.

You needed smarts.

You needed preparation.

I stared at the stack of pink tickets in my hand. Operation Sell Tickets was officially on.

6

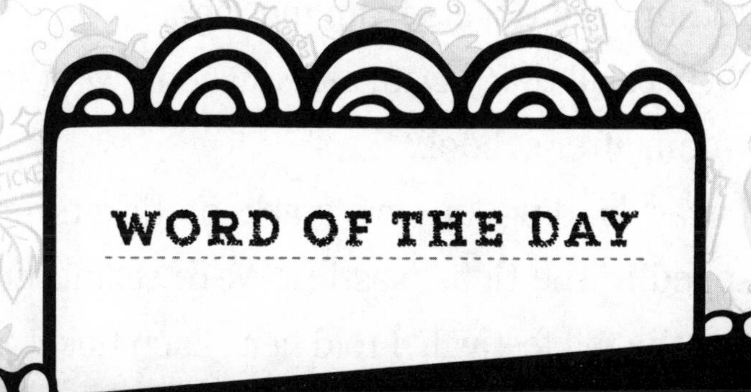

WORD OF THE DAY

STRATEGY

A plan to reach

a goal

The first person I went to sell tickets to was Dadi. She was my best friend at home, after all. And she loved me. She'd buy a hundred tickets from me, right?

"What's all this?" Dadi asked when I went into her room after school.

I was holding up my stack of tickets, still wrapped in the tight plastic. "We're selling tickets for the fall festival," I told her. "Each ticket is a dollar."

"Will there be drums and music?" Dadi asked. "Elephants?"

"Er," I said. "Music, maybe. Drums, probably not. Elephants, definitely not!"

"Too bad," Dadi said. "I saw a festival like that once when I was a little girl."

I grinned. I wish our fall festival could have drums and parades and elephants. That sounded like the best kind of festival. "Sorry, Dadi," I said. "This one will have food and games."

Dadi sighed and pointed to her closet. "Get me my purse."

I ran and fetched her purse. It was a giant brown bag, big enough to put a couch inside. Also, very heavy. "What's in here?" I asked, fiddling with the zipper.

She grabbed it from me. "None of your business," she said. "You never look inside a lady's purse!"

I frowned. "Why?"

"Because it's private." Dadi carefully opened it and took out an ancient-looking coin purse. She counted out some coins and handed them to me. "Here," she said.

“That’s it?” There was no way this was a hundred dollars.

“Count them,” she told me.

I poked at the coins. There were two quarters, four dimes, a nickel, and six pennies. “Keep the change,” Dadi said, smiling.

My mouth opened and shut. “This . . . this is one dollar!” I finally gasped.

“And one penny extra.”

“But . . . I need a hundred dollars. I need to win! And get a prize from the principal . . .”

Dadi frowned. “What prize? You said this was for the fall festival. And I’m only one person, so I need only one ticket!”

I flopped down onto the bed. This was already a disaster! *Deep breaths, Marya!* I told myself.

I remembered what Miss Piccolo had told us. I got up and took Dadi's hands. "You need tickets to buy things at the festival or play the games. Like if you want to bob for apples, you need to pay one ticket. Or if you want to get your face painted, another ticket."

Dadi laughed. "Do I look like the kind of person who bobs for apples?" she asked. "I'm sixty years old, child. I'd fall down and break my hip if I tried that nonsense."

I imagined Dadi in her shalwar kameez and dupatta, bent over a big barrel, looking for apples with her mouth. A giggle slipped out. "Yeah, that sounds awful."

Then she asked, "And what's this about a prize from the principal?"

I flopped back onto the bed and told her everything. How Alexa won the party dress competition at the pumpkin patch, and how I wanted to win something instead of my archenemy for once. Just once. "I've never drunk out of coconuts with straws, Dadi!" I complained. "Never!"

Dadi frowned. "What coconuts?"

"Never mind," I said. "Nobody understands."

"Seems like you're trying to compete with Alexa again," she said.

"Story of my life," I groaned. I closed my eyes and tried to relax. Normally, I'd pretend I was at the beach, but right now that made me feel mad again. So I imagined myself flying in the sky on a magic carpet, like the stories Dadi sometimes told me. I imagined myself very high. Maybe I'd fly over Alexa's house and wave at her.

That would show her.

Dadi poked me in the arm. When I opened my eyes again, she took out some more money from her giant purse. "This is all I have," she said.

It was a ten-dollar bill. I jumped up. "Thank you, Dadi!" I yelled.

She shook her head. "Not so loud! I may be sixty, but I can hear just fine!"

"Sorry." I ripped the plastic from my stack of tickets and counted out ten. "Here you go!"

She grumbled under her breath as she took the tickets from me. "This better be the best festival I've ever been to!"

In my room that night, I counted out my ten dollars plus the coins Dadi had given me. I tore out a piece of paper from my notebook and wrote TICKET SALES on top in very pretty handwriting. Then below it, I wrote DADI and $11.01.

When you were trying to win, you needed every cent.

I looked at my ticket stack. There were still so many left. I needed a plan of action. A strategy.

That meant figuring out how to get to a goal. Aka, Marya Khan, winner.

Ooh, maybe there would be a crown. And a sash. Maybe Principal Cleveland would announce on the loudspeaker: *Marya Khan, Miss Ticket Winner!*

I sighed. Wouldn't that be amazing?

Then I went back to my plan.

The best thing about money was, it was all math. And I was a math whizz. I started to subtract in my head. One hundred minus eleven was the same as one hundred minus ten minus one. I decided to forget about that extra dollar Dadi had given me for now. Basically, I needed ninety more dollars to sell the whole stack.

Ugh, ninety dollars was a big deal. I needed more strategy.

I could ask one person to buy ninety tickets. That would be ninety dollars. That was a lot of money for one person.

Or I could ask nine people to buy ten tickets each. That was only ten dollars each. That didn't seem like too much.

Or I could ask ninety people to buy one ticket each. Yikes, that was too many people!

Where would I find ninety people who wanted to go to a fall festival at Harold Smithers Elementary?

7

WORD OF THE DAY

RUTHLESS

Showing no mercy

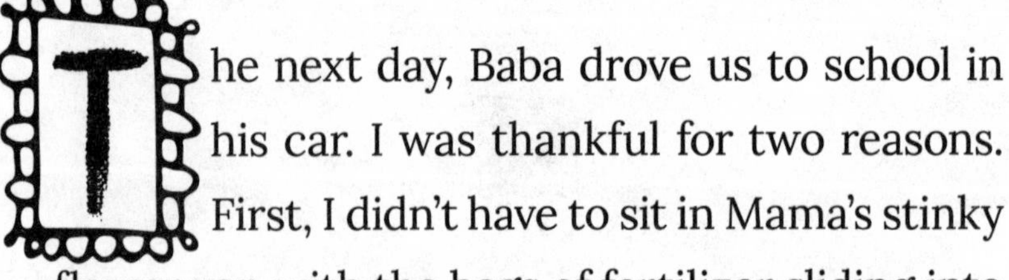

The next day, Baba drove us to school in his car. I was thankful for two reasons. First, I didn't have to sit in Mama's stinky flower van with the bags of fertilizer sliding into me at every turn.

Second, this was the perfect time to ask Baba for money.

"Baba dearest," I began with my best smile.

He gave me a suspicious look in the mirror. "What is it, Marya jaan?"

"I'm guessing she wants something," Aliyah said from the front seat.

I ignored her. "Baba, you know I need to sell tickets for the fall festival," I said. "Would you be so wonderful and kind as to buy ninety?"

"Wonderful and kind?" Baba smiled knowingly. "How much are these tickets, eh?"

I shrugged. "Only a dollar each. A very good deal, if you ask me."

Sal laughed beside me. "That's ninety dollars!"

"I know, Salman dear!" I replied, trying not to get annoyed.

"Ooh, calling your big brother by his full name," Baba teased. "You must be serious about this festival."

If I were standing up, I'd stomp my foot. But since I was sitting in a car, I just gave Baba my best grumpy look. "Focus, Baba. I need to sell tickets! It's for charity!"

"Which charity?" Baba asked.

"It's an animal shelter," I said. "They shelter animals."

Baba frowned. "Do you even know what that means? What does a shelter actually do?"

I gulped, because let's face it: I had no idea. "Well . . ." I started.

Aliyah turned around in her seat. "Tell the

truth, Marya. You don't care about the charity. There's something else up your sleeve!"

I gritted my teeth. Did my siblings exist only to annoy me? "I already told you. The student who sells the most tickets gets a prize." I held up a hand. "And don't ask me what the prize is. I don't know."

Sal hooted. "I hope it's something cool, like fake vomit. Or a fart cushion!"

I ignored his very stupid ideas and tapped Baba's shoulder. "Can you please buy my tickets?" I begged. "I need to win this thing! I really need to!"

He looked at me in the mirror again. "Need to?" he asked.

I nodded so fast, my hair flew all over my face. "Yup!"

Aliyah held up a hand. "Wait, how come Sal isn't begging like you? He's in the same school. Doesn't he have to sell tickets?"

I rolled my eyes, because I didn't care about Sal right now. Or in general. Then suddenly I got scared, because what if he started asking Baba for money too? That would be a disaster.

"Nah," Sal said. "I don't care about ticket sales."

"Not even for the animal shelter?" Baba asked.

Sal shrugged. "I've got my Eid money saved. I'll make a donation on behalf of the Khan family."

Baba and Aliyah looked impressed. Me, not so much. The shelter was very far from my thoughts right now. Should I care about animals? Probably. Should I care more about winning? Definitely!

The car came to a stop outside Aliyah's school.

"So, Baba, what do you think?" I asked.

Baba sighed and turned to face me. “Okay, I’ll buy some tickets,” he replied.

I did a *yay*! touchdown just like Miss Piccolo. It looked good, even though I was sitting down.

Baba held up his pointer finger. “*Some* tickets!” he repeated sternly.

“How many?” I asked.

“How about twenty?” Baba said. “And I want you to ask everyone else in the family too. This will be a good learning experience for you.”

I nodded again. “I already sold ten tickets to Dadi,” I told him proudly.

"Good. Ask your mama as well."

I groaned. Mama was going to be hard to convince. Last week, I asked her to buy me a super-sized caramel popcorn with heavy butter from the grocery store and she said no. Something about rotting teeth. "Sure," I muttered. "I'll try."

Sal nudged me. "Good luck."

"You're gonna need it!" Aliyah said, smirking. She opened the door and stepped out.

I quickly rolled down my window and stuck out my head. "Will you buy some tickets too?" I asked, smiling very big.

She narrowed her eyes and gave me an evil witch look. "I'll think about it."

In class, all the kids were talking about selling tickets. "I'm gonna ask my parents to buy a bunch," Antonio said.

"Me too!" Omar said. "And all my mom's friends too!"

I froze. Did everyone make up their ticket strategy overnight?

Alexa flipped her hair. "I'll get my dad to buy the whole stack," she promised with a big smile. "A hundred tickets is no big deal for a guy like him!"

My heart sank. She was right. Alexa's dad was rich, and he could buy all the tickets in the world. If I wanted to win, I had to do better.

I had to be ruthless. Like a pirate, only using money instead of swords.

"Marya, why are you looking so angry?" Hanna whispered in my ear.

I tried to relax in my chair. "Nothing. Just trying to figure something out."

"Is it about Operation Sell Tickets?" she asked, wiggling her eyebrows.

I looked up very quickly. Both Hanna and Alexa were staring at me.

"How many did you sell so far, Marya?" Alexa asked.

I shrugged. "It's a secret. How many have you sold?"

"It's a secret too!"

Hanna sighed. "You two are being very silly. We're supposed to be doing this for charity. Not to compete against each other."

I didn't say anything, because guess what? Competing against Alexa sounded like the perfect strategy.

8

WORD OF THE DAY

EMPLOYEE

Someone hired
to do a job

All day in school, I wondered about Aliyah. She said she'd think about buying tickets. That didn't mean yes or no. It meant maybe.

Maybe was my least favorite word.

Was she going to torture me? Was she going to make me beg? Was she going to torture me and make me beg and then say no?

The suspense was killing me.

"What's wrong?" Hanna asked at recess. We were both on the swings, our heads back, legs in the air. It was supposed to be fun, but I was too busy worrying about Aliyah.

"Nothing," I replied. "How many tickets did you sell so far?"

She shrugged. "None yet. I got busy with my little sister. She was sick last night and my mom needed help taking care of her."

"You're lucky," I said, sighing. "Little sisters are way better than big sisters."

"Not if you have to clean up their vomit."

Ew. Gross, gross, gross.

I must've had a horrible look on my face, because Hanna laughed at me. "It was only one time. Don't worry, I washed my hands afterward."

I jumped off the swing and literally ran away from her. I had enough problems of my own. I didn't need to think about Hanna's baby sister's vomit.

Gross.

After school, I trudged to Aliyah's room. I peeked inside, not sure if I was allowed to enter. There was a sign saying ENTRY STRICTLY FORBIDDEN on her door.

She was sitting cross-legged on the floor, surrounded by her things. Lots and lots of things.

"What a mess!" I cried. Then I clapped my hand over my mouth, because I probably shouldn't insult her when I wanted something.

"Go away, Marya," Aliyah said, narrowing her eyes at me.

I stepped inside. "I . . . I meant to say, how are you?" I stammered.

"Sure you did." Aliyah gave me another one of her evil smiles.

I decided to get it over with before she put a hex on me. "So, about those tickets . . . ?"

"I'm not even going to come to your stupid festival," Aliyah said. "Why would I need tickets?"

"Um, for the animal shelter?" I almost made a *yay!* touchdown, then decided maybe that wasn't a good idea. Animal shelters were sad, weren't they?

Actually, I didn't know. I'd never been inside one before.

"Really?" Aliyah said, looking totally unimpressed. "I hate animals."

Of course she did. She wasn't human, probably.

"Okay." My shoulders slumped and I got ready to leave. Aliyah wasn't going to buy any tickets. I'd have to figure out something else.

"Wait!"

I turned around. Aliyah had that evil grin on her face again. "You need money, and I need something from you. Like an exchange!"

"What do you need from me?" I asked very slowly. I already knew it was going to be something bad.

Aliyah shrugged. "Nothing much. Just tidy up my room, clean my shoes, organize my closet . . . that sort of thing. I'll buy tickets from you in return."

"How many?" I asked.

She tapped her chin like she was thinking

hard. I waited. Finally, she said, "Thirty. For the whole day on Saturday."

"So basically, you want me to be your employee?"

"If you say so." She shooed me out of her room. "Now leave. Come back tomorrow."

Aliyah turned out to be the worst employer in the history of the world. First of all, her room was a pigsty. Don't get me wrong, I already knew this. I couldn't remember how many times I'd sneaked inside to "borrow" something of hers. But cleaning a pigsty is a very different thing.

There were clothes, books, and shoes scattered all over. Plus, empty wrappers from all the snacks she ate, even though Mama didn't allow snacks in our bedrooms. There was a spot on the carpet where she'd spilled soda or something.

Then I remembered Hanna's sister and wondered if the spot was actually vomit.

How could one person make such a big mess?

"Here are your cleaning supplies," Aliyah said, handing me a plastic bag.

I looked inside. There was cleaning spray, a roll of paper towels, and a toothbrush. "What's this for?" I asked, taking out the toothbrush.

"For my shoes," she replied, and then cackled like a witch.

I stared at her in horror. "Shoes?"

She picked up her Nikes and dangled them in my face. "They need to be shiny!"

I gritted my teeth. *Thirty tickets. Thirty tickets*, I kept repeating in my head as I got to work.

Here were my tasks as Aliyah Khan's employee:

Step 1: Pick up all the clothes and throw them into the laundry basket. Don't forget to pinch your nose with one hand, because some of the clothes smelled horrible.

Step 2: Throw all the wrappers in the trash. Even the ones with snacks still inside them, because they looked about a hundred years old.

Step 3: Straighten everything on the desk.

Step 4: Pick up all the books from the floor and line them neatly on the bookshelf.

Step 5: Take a break. If the witch sister starts scolding you, tell her the US government allows breaks.

Step 6: Spray cleaner on every single surface and scrub with paper towels. This goes for the spot of soda on the carpet too.

Step 7: Flop on the bed and demand your money.

"You didn't clean my shoes!" Aliyah reminded me. She'd been sitting on a chair the whole time, watching me.

"But I've been doing this for hours!" I whined. "My arms hurt and my eyes itch."

"Nobody told you to spray so much cleaner," Aliyah said, smirking. "You're only supposed to use a tiny bit."

"For normal rooms," I replied. "This is an epic disaster zone that needs to be covered in chemicals."

Aliyah growled. "Shoes! Now!"

I dragged myself off the bed and picked up the toothbrush. "There better not be any vomit on your shoes!"

gloss
cream

9

IMPRESSIVE

Having a long-lasting effect

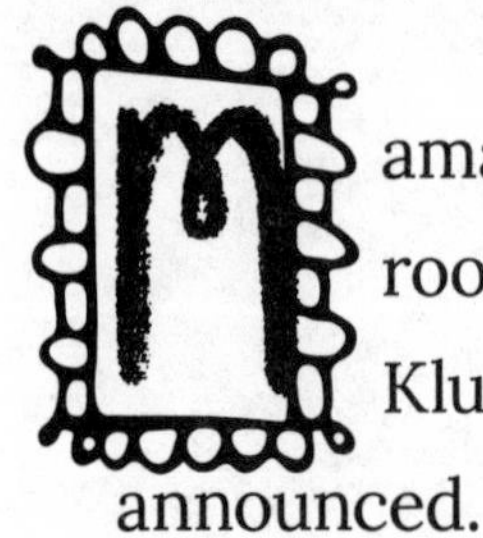

ama was really happy that Aliyah's room was clean. "We're going to Klucky Chicken Palace for dinner!" she announced.

I groaned because I was so tired. But then I realized I was also very hungry. "Can Hanna come too?" I asked. If I had to eat with Aliyah, aka my boss, I should at least have my best friend with me.

"Good idea," Mama said. "Let me call Hanna's mom and invite them."

When we reached Klucky, Hanna's family was already there. I grinned when I saw her little sister, Sana, looking adorable in a pink-and-white romper. "Hey, cutie." I waved.

Sana waved back with both arms.

"You look exhausted," Hanna whispered.

"Tell me about it," I replied, sitting down very slowly.

"Marya cleaned Aliyah's room!" Mama told everyone proudly.

"Yeah," Sal added. "We're celebrating the fact that we can see Aliyah's carpet now."

Aliyah glared at him. "Shut up!" she hissed.

Hanna giggled. "I can't wait until Sana is old enough to clean my room."

"Don't forget the shoes," I muttered. "With a toothbrush."

Aliyah was getting madder. "It's not like Marya was being nice or anything," she said. "I paid her. It was a job!"

"Really?" Hanna's mom, Mrs. Gamal, turned to me. "That's impressive."

I shrugged. "I'm pretty impressive," I agreed.

Sal howled with laughter. Aliyah just glared at me again. If she wasn't careful, her eyes would stay narrow like that and she'd never be able to open them wide again.

Baba and Mr. Gamal went to order. I was so tired, I almost fell asleep. Only, Mrs. Gamal started talking about the fall festival, which woke me right back up. "My hospital staff is very excited about it," she said. "They're all moms, and they want to take their kids as a group. I'm going to have to give them the day off."

"They'll be very thankful," Mama said.

"You'll be impressive, Mrs. Gamal," I said.

Hanna's mom smiled. "Well, that's true."

Then I thought of something. "Wait, how did your staff know about our festival?"

"It was in the local paper," she replied. "Your principal must have sent in a notice about it."

Hanna and I looked at each other. The local paper? That meant the fall festival would be bigger than just Harold Smithers Elementary. It would be big enough for the whole town.

"You know what this means, right?" I whispered to Hanna.

"No, what?" Hanna asked.

"More people means more tickets," I explained.

Just then, Baba and Mr. Gamal came back with trays of food. I grabbed some chicken nuggets and fries.

"How much money did you collect so far?" Hanna asked me.

From my jeans pocket I fished out a paper where I'd written my sales numbers. "Let's see," I said. "Dadi, ten dollars. Baba, twenty dollars. Aliyah, thirty dollars. That makes sixty dollars total."

Hanna's eyes grew big. "That's a lot. You've almost sold all hundred."

I shrugged. One hundred minus sixty was forty. I said, "Not really. There's still forty dollars left."

"How do you do math so fast in your head?" she asked.

"No big deal," I replied. But secretly I thought it was pretty impressive.

On Sunday morning, I decided to be brave and ask Mama about Operation Sell Tickets. "I just need forty more dollars, Mama," I begged. "Then I'll have sold the entire stack."

"Forty dollars is a lot of money, Marya," Mama said. She was putting on her hijab in front of the hallway mirror. It was almost time for her to leave for work.

"I won't eat at Klucky Chicken Palace for a whole month," I promised. "And I won't beg for any snacks when we go to the Pakistani store. Not even a single packet of spicy chips!"

Mama looked like she didn't believe me. "You love those spicy chips."

It was true. I really loved them. But I'd give them up for a few weeks if it meant winning a trophy.

Or, you know, whatever prize I got. I wasn't picky at this point.

I joined my hands together like a prayer. "Please, Mama? Pretty please?"

Mama sighed. "Okay, I'll give you twenty dollars if you help me in the flower shop today."

More work? What was the matter with my family, expecting me to work for money? But twenty dollars was half of my final goal, so I guessed it was worth it. "Ugh, fine," I said. "But I refuse to touch any fertilizer."

Helping out at Mama's flower shop wasn't bad, except for one big problem: Alexa.

"What's she doing here?" I asked, staring at the blond girl in the blue-and-white striped dress. We were standing in the alley behind the shop, where

Mama's van was parked. I was on one side. Alexa was on the other. Mama was in the middle, her hands on her hips.

Mama gave me a look that said, *You'd better behave, Marya Khan.* "Alexa's mom called me for a flower order and I mentioned that you were helping me today," Mama explained.

"So . . . ?" I still didn't understand how Alexa had ended up at the shop with us.

"So . . . I might have invited Alexa," Mama said, shrugging like it was no big deal.

She was wrong. It was a very big deal! "But why?" I sputtered.

Mama's *behave* look got even more stern. "Marya, she's your neighbor and classmate. And she's a great girl."

"Well, two of those things are true," I grumbled.

Alexa came over and smiled brightly. "What do you need us to do, Mrs. Khan?" she asked.

Mama pointed to the back of her van. "All these plants need to be taken inside."

I waited. "What else?"

Mama looked puzzled. "Nothing else, that's it."

I blinked. When Aliyah told me she had work for me to do, she'd given me one million tasks. "Are you sure?"

"Do you *want* more work?" Mama asked.

"Er, no." I closed my mouth and walked over to the van. It was full of cute little plants in little clay pots.

"Ooh, mint," Alexa said from behind me, breathing deeply.

I grabbed a plant in each hand and headed to the shop. Alexa copied me. "This is easy!" she said. Only, her hands trembled a little, and soil flew around her. Some of it landed on her dress.

She put down her plants and rubbed at her dress. The muddy patch just got worse.

I couldn't help it. I giggled. "You look totally goofy!"

Alexa gasped. Then she picked up a piece of dirt and threw it at me. "You too!"

The dirt landed somewhere on my head, and I giggled harder. Then Alexa started giggling too. It was strange. I never would have thought it would be funny to move plants with my archenemy.

Or fun.

I definitely never thought it would be fun.

It took an hour to bring all the plants inside and set them on the shelves. It would've taken less time, only I was telling fertilizer jokes and Alexa kept laughing and dropping soil everywhere. We both were totally goofy.

Mama made us sweep the shop floor. When we were done, she handed us water bottles, plus forty dollars each.

"Thanks," I said, my eyes nearly popping out of my head. She'd only promised me twenty. This was double.

Mama smiled and winked. "For getting along so well with Alexa."

I quickly counted in my head. I already had sixty tickets. Forty more meant one hundred.

I'd sold the entire pack of tickets Miss Piccolo had given me.

I did a little *yay!* touchdown in my heart.

Or more like a hundred touchdowns.

10

WORD OF THE DAY

BIZARRE

Something strange or wild

On Monday morning, Principal Cleveland called a special assembly. "We have some special guests with us today," he said in his booming voice.

I looked around. All I could hear were kids.

Oh, and barking. Why was there barking?

A man came up to the front. He was pulling a big white dog on a leash.

"Oh, how cute!" Hanna squealed.

Actually, the entire cafeteria was squealing.

A woman followed, holding a crate in her arms. She knelt on the ground and opened the crate. Out tumbled four little kittens. They were cute and cuddly and furry.

The squeals in the cafeteria became even louder.

What was going on? Since when had our school become a zoo? This was totally bizarre.

The woman stood up. "We're from the animal shelter," she said loudly. "We wanted you to meet some of the animals you'll be helping with your fall festival."

I don't think anyone was listening. The man with the dog was going around the cafeteria, letting kids pet it. Everyone was super excited, which made the dog bark even louder.

The woman on the stage continued. "That dog is Luka," she said. "He was abandoned when he was born. We found him on the street, scared and hungry. He was so thin, you could see his ribs."

Okay, I officially melted. I've never been so hungry that my ribs showed. It sounded awful. I wanted to pet Luka, but I wanted to hear his story even more.

The woman kept talking. She told us how the shelter took care of Luka, fed him, and made him all better. Now, they were waiting for someone to adopt him. It was the same with the kittens. They didn't have a mother, so the shelter took care of them too. Made sure they were safe and their bellies were full of food.

"We run on donations," the woman explained. "When you have your fall festival, remember that the money you raise by selling tickets will go to help Luka and these kittens and all their friends."

When we got back to class, Miss Piccolo handed out some worksheets. “We’re going to improve our writing,” she said.

Only I couldn’t focus on the worksheets. I kept thinking about Luka and the kittens and all the other animals at the shelter. They needed lots and lots of money so that their ribs wouldn’t show and their bellies would be full of food.

“What’s the matter?” Hanna whispered. “Worried about your ticket sales?”

I shook my head. “I’m worried about *all* the ticket sales,” I whispered back.

Hanna gave me a weird look. “What do you mean?”

Just then, Miss Piccolo said, “I’m out of markers. I’ll get some from the closet down the hall.”

Alexa raised her hand. “I can be in charge while you’re gone!”

I rolled my eyes. Alexa always wanted to be in charge.

Miss Piccolo smiled gratefully. "Thank you, Alexa. I'll only be a minute."

As soon as she left the room, I stood up. "How many tickets have you all sold?" I asked the class. Okay, I demanded. Loudly.

"Marya!" Alexa gasped. "You have to sit down and be quiet. I'm in charge."

I ignored her. "We have to sell lots of tickets for those cute little animals!" I said, less loudly this

time. “Is everyone doing their job? Is everyone selling tickets?”

Antonio shrugged. “I sold ten tickets.”

Omar nodded. “Twenty-five for me.”

I felt my heart sink. That was it? The festival was only one week away. “You said you’d sell to your entire family!” I said to Antonio.

He shrugged again. “I got busy. I forgot.”

“Me too,” Omar said, hanging his head.

I glared at them both. “How could anyone forget about Luka? And those little kittens who don’t have a mama? They need our help!”

Hanna wrinkled her forehead. “Wait a minute, Marya. I thought you wanted to win the big prize. Since when do you care about Luka?”

I gulped. She was right. Until this morning, I had totally forgotten about the animals too. “Well, I care now,” I told her, crossing my arms over my chest.

“What about Operation Sell Tickets?” she asked.

“It’s still on,” I replied. “But now it’s for everyone.”

The class cheered, even though they didn't know what we were talking about. "How do we sell more tickets?" Omar asked. "I'm not good at asking people for things."

Hanna sighed. "Neither am I."

"Maybe we can make some flyers about the animals?" Alexa suggested. "And we could go around the neighborhood together, in a group. That way nobody needs to feel shy."

Those were actually very good ideas. I gave Alexa a smile. "Let's do it," I said quietly.

"Yay!" She smiled back and held out her arms in a touchdown.

When Miss Piccolo came back, we told her our plan. She shook her head and grumbled about not being able to leave us alone for two minutes. For the record, she'd been gone for five whole minutes.

But she gave us construction paper and crayons. I drew a cat with a bell on its collar, because just like Mama, I liked cats too. Underneath the picture, I wrote, *This kitty needs your help*, with ten exclamation marks.

"Finished!" Alexa called out. I looked over at her flyer. She'd drawn a puppy with big eyes. It was wearing a bell on its collar too. She'd written, *This puppy needs your help*, but with a smiley face instead of exclamation marks.

"Hey, you match!" Hanna said, giggling.

"Mine is better," I said. But I didn't really mean it.

"Great minds think alike," Alexa said. "That's what my mom says anyway."

"Your mom's right," I told her. "We *are* both great minds!"

11

WORD OF THE DAY

A very large group of people

On Friday afternoon, Alexa and I stood outside Mama's flower shop with Baba. "How many kids are coming?" he asked nervously.

"Eight," I replied, even though I'd already told him.

"We need more parents," he grumbled. "I can't handle so many kids."

"Don't worry," I said. "Hanna's dad will be here."

Baba perked up. "Really? Doesn't he have a game today?"

Hanna's dad used to be a soccer player in Egypt. Now he coached the high school soccer

team. They usually had practice games on the weekends.

Alexa shrugged. "Maybe he went out of town."

Baba shook his head. "You can't go out of town when you're coaching a team. It's important to show up."

"Hmm," Alexa said sadly. I knew she was thinking about her dad, who was always out of town.

Then I forgot all about Alexa, because Hanna's car was coming down the road. "There they are!" I shouted.

Mr. Gamal parked the car and Hanna got out, waving madly. Right behind her were Omar and a few other kids from our class. They all lived near Hanna's house, so Mr. Gamal had picked them up.

"Heya!" came Antonio's voice. I turned to see him walking with his big brother, who was in college.

"I'll pick you up in two hours," Antonio's brother said.

Baba counted heads. "One, two, three . . . eight!" He swallowed. "That's quite a horde."

I imagined a group of kids holding up swords and shields, running down the street yelling. I'd be the leader, of course. Queen Marya of the Third-Grade Horde.

Mr. Gamal clapped his hands. "Okay, kids! Ready?"

Everyone held up their flyers. "Ready!" we all shouted. We were here to sell tickets and raise lots of money for the animal shelter.

We needed a strategy, obviously. I told them what to do, because I was the leader. Only Alexa stood right next to me the whole time, nodding like she was saying, *I approve this message.* I ignored her and kept talking.

Step 1: Go to each shop and hand out a flyer.

Step 2: Tell the person at the counter all about the animal shelter and how you are selling tickets for the fall festival. Say this very nicely, or they'll tell you to get lost.

Step 3: Talk about the fall festival. Use words like fabulous and amazing and incredible.

Step 4: If someone buys tickets, say thank you a hundred times.

Step 5: Leave the shop with a big smile. Don't forget to say thank you again.

"Let's go, team!" Alexa said when I'd finished, like *she* was in charge.

I told myself we were cooperating today, so I just smiled and said "Yay!" with everyone.

There were lots of shops and restaurants downtown. We split into two groups, each headed by a dad, and got to work.

Only it wasn't really work. It ended up being

so much fun! I thought people would be mad we'd disturbed them. But it turned out everyone loved animals. And kids. A few ladies cried, "Oh, how cute!" like we were babies.

"Thank you," Alexa replied. She was wearing a white silk dress with a big red bow on the waist, so maybe she thought everyone was talking about her.

I rolled my eyes a lot.

After two hours, we all met back up in front of Mama's shop. "That was so much fun!" Hanna said, laughing.

"Yeah!" Alexa replied. For once, her hair looked all ruffled and messy. And the bow around her waist was now a flowing red ribbon. She reminded me of how she'd looked in Mama's shop when we worked together. Totally goofy.

I helped everyone count their money. Ten, twenty, thirty . . . "OMG!" I squealed. "We sold them all!"

Alexa looked over my shoulder and counted again. "We sold all the tickets," she announced.

I nudged her. "I just said that!"

Alexa put her arm around me and squeezed. "We did it, Marya. Operation Sell Tickets is a success!"

Hanna grabbed my hand from the other side and squeezed too. "Told you we'd get more done if we worked together."

I couldn't help it. I grinned. "We did!"

All the kids started jumping up and down and clapping. Talk about a horde! Baba looked like he wanted to run away. But Mr. Gamal did something really shocking. He took out a whistle from his pocket and blew it loudly.

We all went silent.

"Good job, everyone!" he yelled. "Now, who wants ice cream?"

"Hooray!" Antonio yelled back. I think he was more excited about eating ice cream than selling tickets.

Everyone followed Mr. Gamal to the ice cream shop at the end of the street. Alexa, Hanna, and I went last. "You wanna share an ice cream sundae?" Hanna asked.

"Definitely," Alexa and I said together.

12

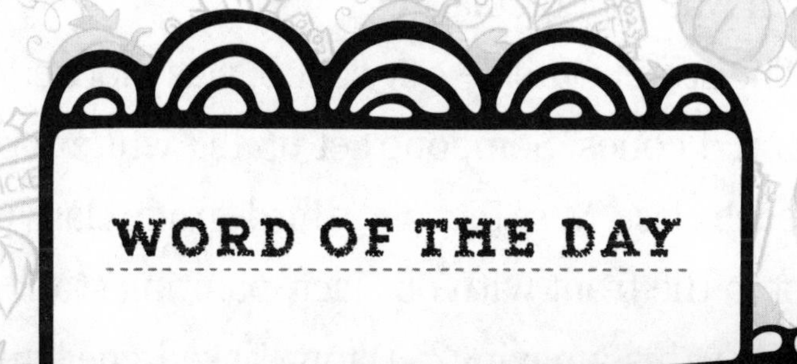

WORD OF THE DAY

ECSTATIC

Extremely happy

On Saturday, two amazing things happened.

The first one was the fall festival, which was spectacular!

The street outside our school was blocked off with red cones. Someone set up big white tables for each class. Miss Piccolo's third-grade class was right in the front with our face-painting station.

"Isn't this amazing?" Hanna asked cheerfully. She was dressed in a painter's smock, a paintbrush tucked behind her ear.

"You look so professional!" Alexa told her. "Like one of those French artists."

She giggled and pretended to twirl a mustache. "Thank you."

I looked around. The fifth graders were setting up Jenga Giant, which was super cool. Sal saw me looking and waved. I waved back.

Fourth grade had set up a dunking booth. "Who do you think we'll get to dunk?" Hanna asked me.

"Principal Cleveland!" Alexa and I both said together. Then we laughed, because it was strange to have the same idea at the same time with someone who was supposed to be your archenemy.

Only today, Alexa didn't really seem like an enemy. Honestly, she hadn't for a long time.

"Just a super-annoying friend," I whispered.

"What's that, Marya?" Alexa asked.

"Nothing." I looked at the other tables. Second grade had a beanbag toss and a ring toss. Kindergarten and first grade had food stalls full of candy corn, brownies, cupcakes, nachos, and soda. "I'm hungry," I announced.

"You can't eat until the festival officially starts," Hanna reminded me.

How unfair! I looked away from the delicious food before I started drooling. Then my eyes popped out of my head at what I saw right in front of me. "A hayride!" I yelled.

Alexa nodded, looking very pleased. "My mom arranged that," she said.

"How come?" I asked.

Alexa shrugged. "I convinced my mom it would be a good photo op."

"Wow," I whispered. Who'd have thought hayrides would be good for the city council?

"Does this mean you're my best friend, Marya Khan?" Alexa whispered back.

"Let's not get carried away," I told her. But I was smiling for some strange reason.

The festival officially opened at ten o'clock. I was happy to see so many people. Parents, teachers, even high school students. There was the old lady who'd pinched my cheeks and called me cute last week. A guy was walking around on stilts, blowing giant bubbles. Two middle-school girls were doing gymnastics on a little stage. My neighbor Mr. Trenton, aka Wizard Caiden, was standing next to his magic truck waving at kids. "Big show at noon!" he cried.

Best of all was a tent set up by the animal

shelter. Luka was there, plus lots of cats in cages. There was even a parrot. A sign on the tent said ADOPT A PET TODAY! and lots of people were lined up to get information.

That made my heart happy. I didn't even care that I hadn't won Operation Sell Tickets, because helping those cutie-pie animals made me feel like a real winner.

Don't get me wrong, winning a beach vacation and drinking coconut juice from a straw would have been awesome.

But this was pretty good too.

From the corner of my eye, I saw Mama and Baba coming toward me. Aliyah and Dadi followed them. "This is wonderful, Marya jaan!" Dadi exclaimed.

I grinned. "I know!"

Aliyah rolled her eyes. "It's fine," she said.

"You have lots of tickets from the time I cleaned your pigsty—er, room," I reminded her. "You can do everything here."

She gave another one of her evil grins. "All I'm

ADOPT A PET
TODAY!

interested in is the dunking booth. I heard they got some middle-school teachers to volunteer!"

Aliyah waved, then led Dadi toward the dunking booth. Mama and Baba went over to the food table.

"Your family is so nice, Marya." Alexa sighed.

I gulped. I didn't really know how to reply, because Alexa's family was the opposite of nice.

Suddenly, Alexa gasped. "I can't believe it!" she whispered.

"What is it?" I looked around. A tall blond man in a suit was coming straight at us. It was Alexa's dad.

Alexa broke out into a beautiful smile.

I blinked. I didn't know she could smile like that. Like an angel with a ray of sunshine coming out of her.

"Hi, honey!" Mr. Rhodes said, waving.

"I thought you were in New York," Alexa said.

He wrapped his arm around her. "I heard that the Harold Smithers fall festival is *the* place to be this year!"

Alexa continued to smile like some character in a comic book. I think she'd forgotten how to speak in her shock.

I nudged her, but she didn't move. I was starting to get a little freaked out. Then I thought about Baba and how I'd feel if he were never around. And then how happy I'd be if he suddenly showed up at the school festival.

I'd be ecstatic, that's what.

"All students, report behind the stage!" Principal Cleveland's voice boomed out.

It was the end of the festival, and I was exhausted. I was also super full of junk food. The best part? I'd gone on six hayrides. Six!

In other words, I was super happy.

And now, we were getting to the second amazing thing of the day.

Principal Cleveland was holding a piece of paper in his hand. When everyone had gathered, he said: "You all worked really hard today! The

festival was spectacular, and we raised a lot of money for the animal shelter!"

We all clapped. "Woo-hoo!" I yelled.

Principal Cleveland continued. "And now for the winner of our little competition."

I froze, because I'd totally forgotten about the prize.

"The student who sold the most tickets was . . ."

My heart thumped in my chest, even though I knew it wouldn't be me. I'd given up on Operation Sell Tickets to help my class, and I was okay with that. The animals were way more important.

Only, I wanted to win so badly. I wanted Principal Cleveland to announce my name. I didn't even care what the prize was. I just wanted to win.

Hanna's hand slipped into mine and squeezed tight. I grabbed Alexa's hand with my other one and also squeezed. "Well?" I finally demanded.

Principal Cleveland cleared his throat. "Actually, we didn't have a clear winner, because one class worked together to sell tickets, rather than individually." He looked right at me. "Miss Piccolo told me all about it. Her third-grade class raised five times more than the rest of the school, so they've *all* won!"

I blinked. "I don't understand," I said. "We all won?"

"Yes," he replied, smiling.

"What did we win?" Alexa asked.

"A pizza party at Marco's."

I broke into a huge smile. This was perfect! My entire class got to win together! And we raised so much money for Luka and his friends. *Yay!* touchdown times a million!

Also, I just remembered I didn't really like coconuts. Pizza was way more delicious.

Miss Piccolo smiled at me. "Your strategy was a success, Marya Khan."

I just grinned.

Hanna and I hugged each other. Omar and Antonio whooped loudly. Mama, Baba, and Dadi kept clapping. Even Aliyah smiled, which was basically a miracle.

Alexa turned to me. "Can't wait for our pizza party!" She threw her arms around me, but I didn't even mind.

Now it's your turn! Bake these Simple Pumpkin Spice Cookies with the help of a grown-up.

Ingredients

1 package spice cake mix
1 can solid-pack pumpkin
raisins or chocolate chips (optional)

Instructions

1. Preheat oven to 350°F.
2. In a bowl, mash the cake mix and pumpkin together with a fork. Add raisins or chocolate chips, if desired.
3. Spray a cookie sheet lightly with vegetable oil spray.
4. Drop medium-sized spoonfuls of the mixture onto the cookie tray. Do not flatten.
5. Bake 10 to 15 minutes.
6. Allow cookies to cool before eating.

ABOUT THE AUTHOR AND ILLUSTRATOR

Saadia Faruqi was born in Pakistan and moved to the United States when she was twenty-two years old. She writes the Yasmin series and popular middle-grade novels such as *Yusuf Azeem Is Not a Hero*. Besides writing books for kids, she also loves reading, binge-watching her favorite shows, and taking naps. She lives in Houston with her family.

Ani Bushry graduated from the University of West England with a background in graphic design and illustration. She grew up listening to stories her mom told her and always wanted to tell her own. She lives in the Maldives with her husband and cat, Lilo, whom she loves to spoil.